AARTI'S WORKBOOK

English Activity Book

LET'S LEARN WITH FUN

First Edition: June 2021

Typeset in Helvetica

ISBN: 978-93-91116-71-2

Cover Design : Debabrata Sahoo

Publisher: StoryMirror Infotech Pvt. Ltd.
                145, First Floor, Powai Plaza, Hiranandani Gardens,
                Powai, Mumbai - 400076, India

Web: https://storymirror.com
Facebook: https://facebook.com/storymirror
Twitter: https://twitter.com/story_mirror
Instagram: https://instagram.com/storymirror
Email: marketing@storymirror.com

"Known to Unknown method" and "Trial and error method" is helps every child to learn each and every concepts.. Child will always try to do all of the easy worksheets first, then they will try for difficult one.In this way Children will learn to solve worksheets by themselves.This book is made for 3 to 6 years children so that after solving this worksheets children learn to concentrate on what they do for longer periods and busy in positive way. Children's short term and long term memory will improve. Child will understand the different concepts of solving worksheets.By engaging kids in brain teasers, will help to enhance various critical skill-sets like critical thinking, problem-solving, and creativity.Logic skills can be easily strengthened of a child with daily practice. When they solve these exercises regularly. In addition to solving the overall problem, parents can set time how long it takes to solve the problem by their child. You can time each of the smaller puzzles so that the child can see how much they have improved and where they still need work. You can even turn it into a competition, so that children can see how they measure up to others in the class. If it is a competition, make sure that it stays on friendly terms by giving out stars,smiley, Good Remarks by which children will feel happy and want to solve it again and again.

W
X
A
C
B
Q
Z
F
E
G
H
T
D
I
K
J
R
L
M
N
S
V
U
P
O

a c j b e d f i
g k h l n p m o
q t r s w u x v z y

M _______   k _______   R ______

V _______   f ______   O ______

S ______   p ______   Q _____

D _____   h _______   E _____

What comes in between :-

B ____ D   s _____ u

M ____ O   g _____ i

S ____ U   f ____ h

H ____ J   r _____ t

K ____ M   b _____ d

What comes before:-

____ L   ____ m

____ J   ____ s

____ G   ____ p

____ D   ____ h

[jug, lotus, ball, dustbin, apple, fish, ice-cream, kite]

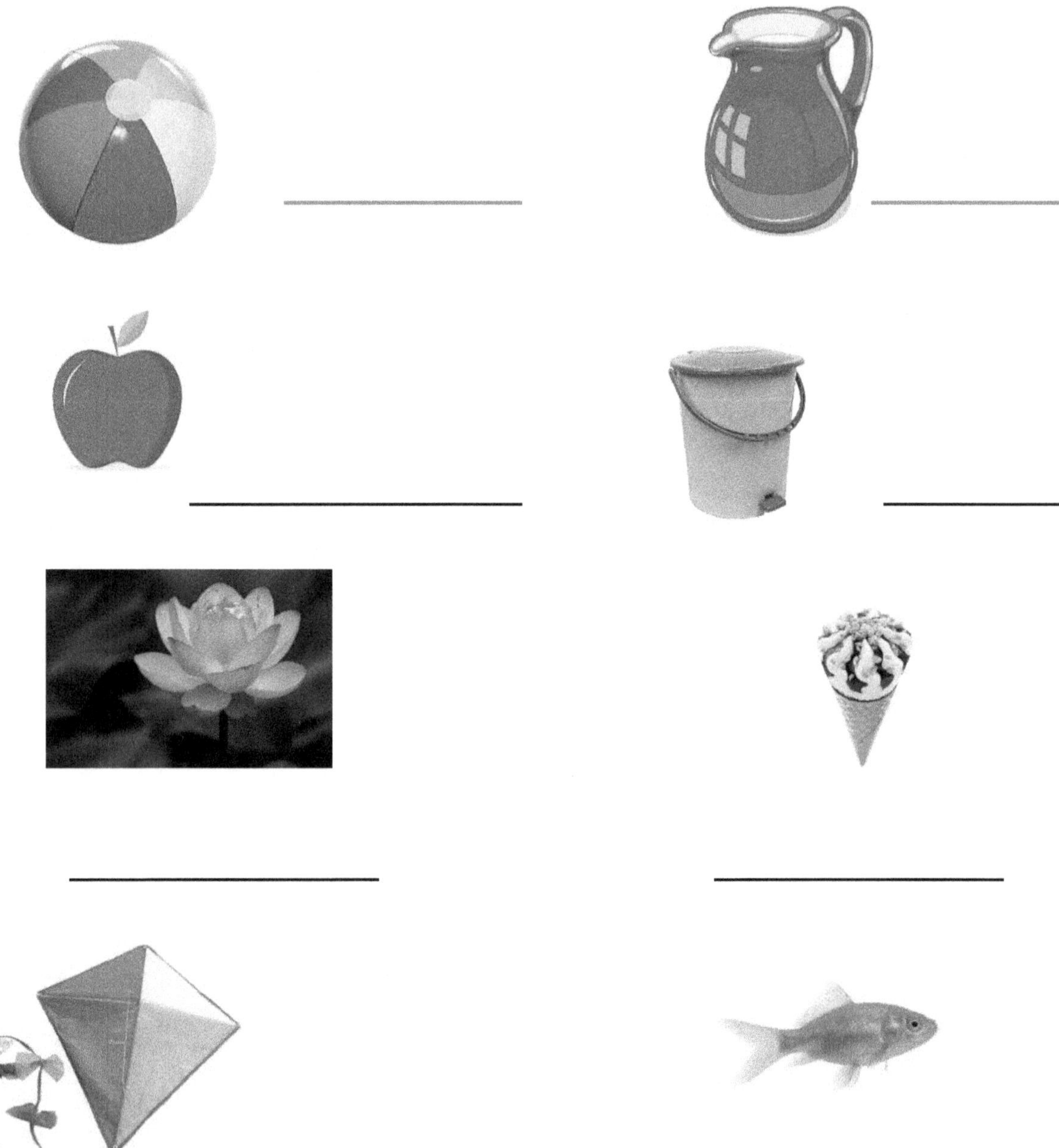

	mat	hat	run	fat
	bun	fun	sun	mad
3.	fit	bun	sit	hit
	man	fan	ran	cut
	cot	hot	fun	not
	bag	fat	tag	rag
	net	pet	bet	fan
	day	say	bat	ray
9.	bin	man	pin	tin
	heat	book	hook	took

hand

car

bun

say

house

head

book

mat

sun

ray

band

jar

hook

rat

mouse

shed

top - _______________

book - _______________

hen - _______________

pen - _______________

pot - _______________

hand - _______________

7] pencil - _______________

8] leg - _______________

b	v	f	h	f	c	a	t	r
	u	t	m	n	d	s	g	x
	y	d	o	g	v	b	a	y
w	p	s	u	n	l	s	p	j
	b	u	s	f	i	v	p	m
	c	x	z	r	o	n	l	n
	f	u	l	t	n	s	e	m
	u	m	b	r	e	l	l	a

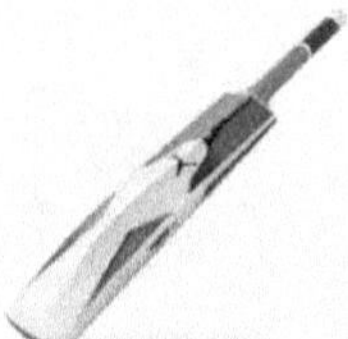

____________ umbrella

____________ apple

____________ orange

____________ hand

____________ sunflower

____________ lamp

____________ onion

____________ cat

____________ house

ice-cream

Box "A"

mat	mop
man	lip
cot	box
bee	sun

Box "B"

fox	tip
hot	top
cat	see
bun	fan

Box A – B

____

____

____

____

____

____

____

____

1] Comfortable   ________________

2] Fold - ________________

   Peacock - ________________

   Woman - ________________

   Sudden - ________________

   Cupboard - ________________

7] Rabbit - ________________

   Coconut - ________________

   Broad - ________________

10] Bring - ________________

• Circle the naming words or nouns:-

shy	mother	old	park
beautiful	pencil	lion	found
father	going	ball	school
tiger	laugh	Delhi	lot
	teacher		

example: ball + owl + apple + table = boat

1] shop + hot + ice + pen = ______________________

2] carrot + ant + rabbit = ______________________

3] bat + umbrella + sun = ______________________

4] top + rat + axe + ink + nose = ______________________

5] sweet + cow + oil + offer + tap + egg + ram =

____

6] arrow + eat + row + oil + pot + lit + axe + net + egg

____

	"A"	**"B"**
	fast	sky
2]	hot	ice-cream
3]	blue	train
4]	cold	tea
5]	sweet	grass
	sharp	mango
7]	green	knife
8]	spicy	lemon
	sour	egg
10]	boiled	chilli

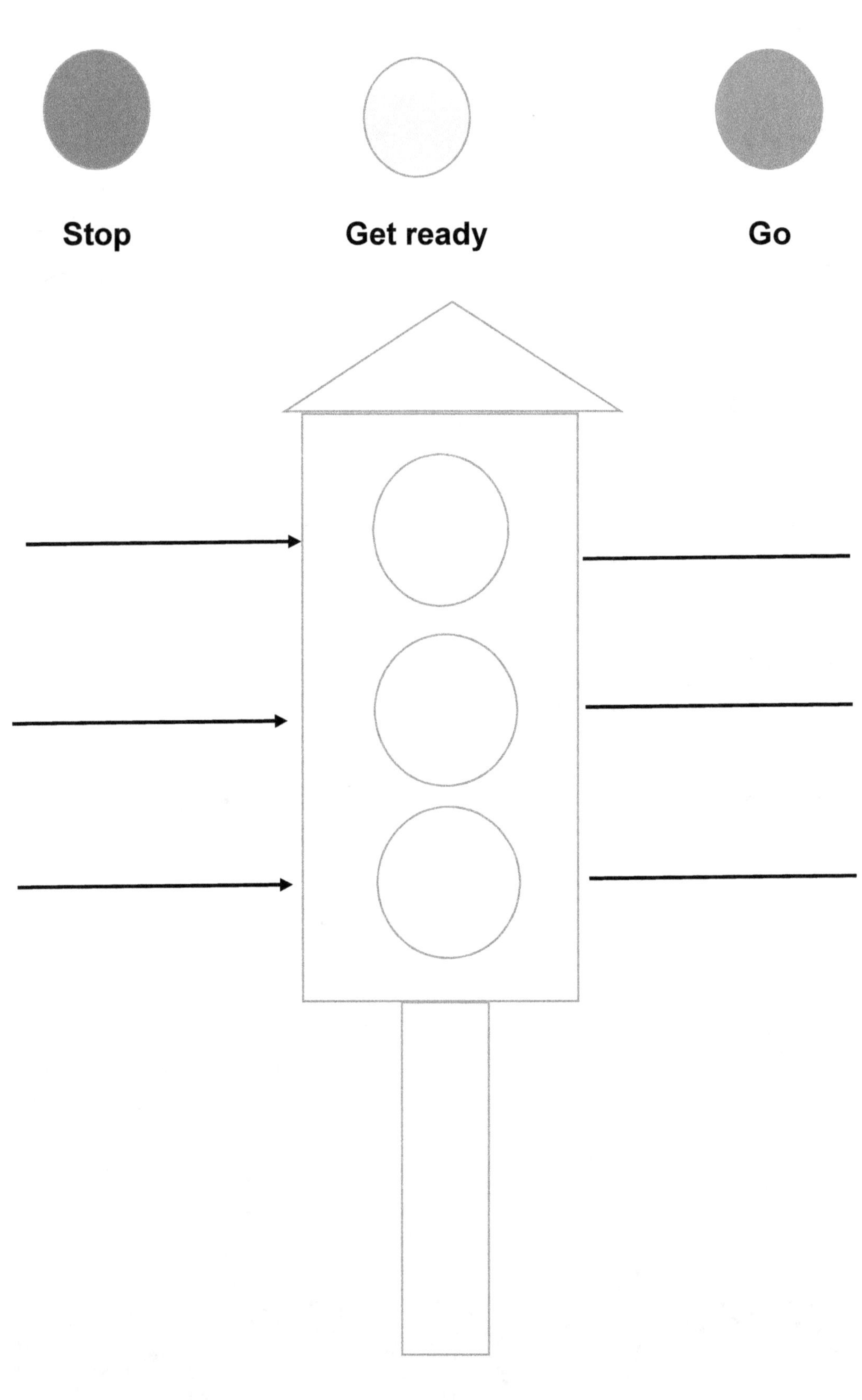

Stop
Get ready
Go

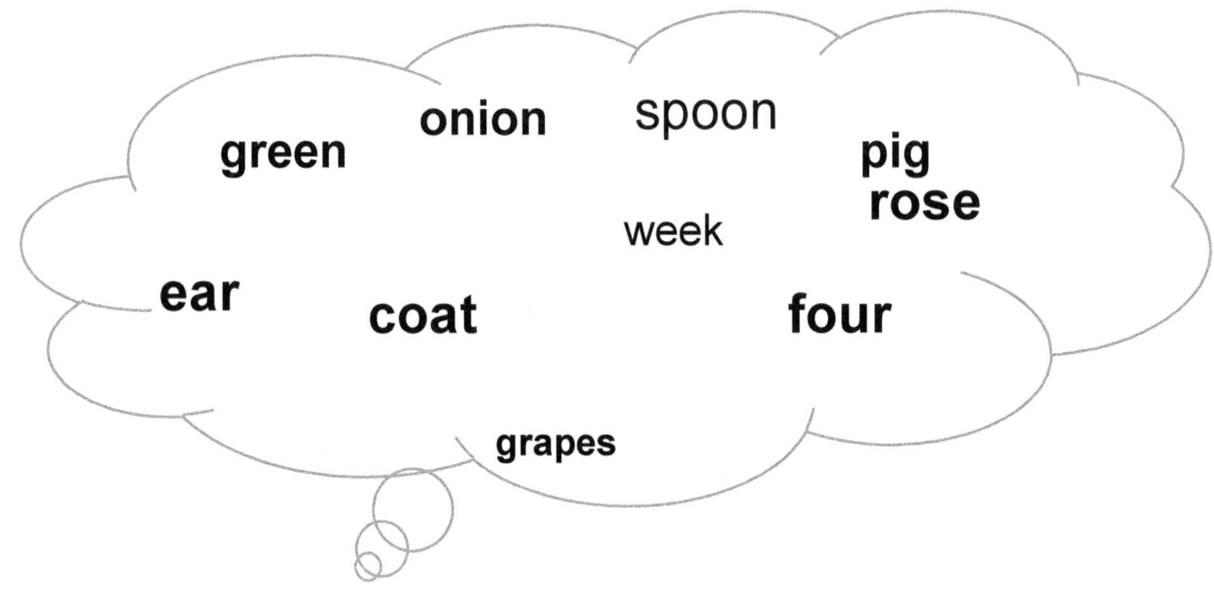

Nose, eye, chin, ___________________

Day, month, year, ___________________

Cat, dog, horse, ___________________

4] Red, yellow, blue, ___________________

Shirt, pant, tie, ___________________

Six, nine, one, ___________________

Bowl, plate, frying pan, ___________________

Apple, banana, cherry, ___________________

Shoe flower, jasmine, lily, ___________________

Tomato, potato, chilli,

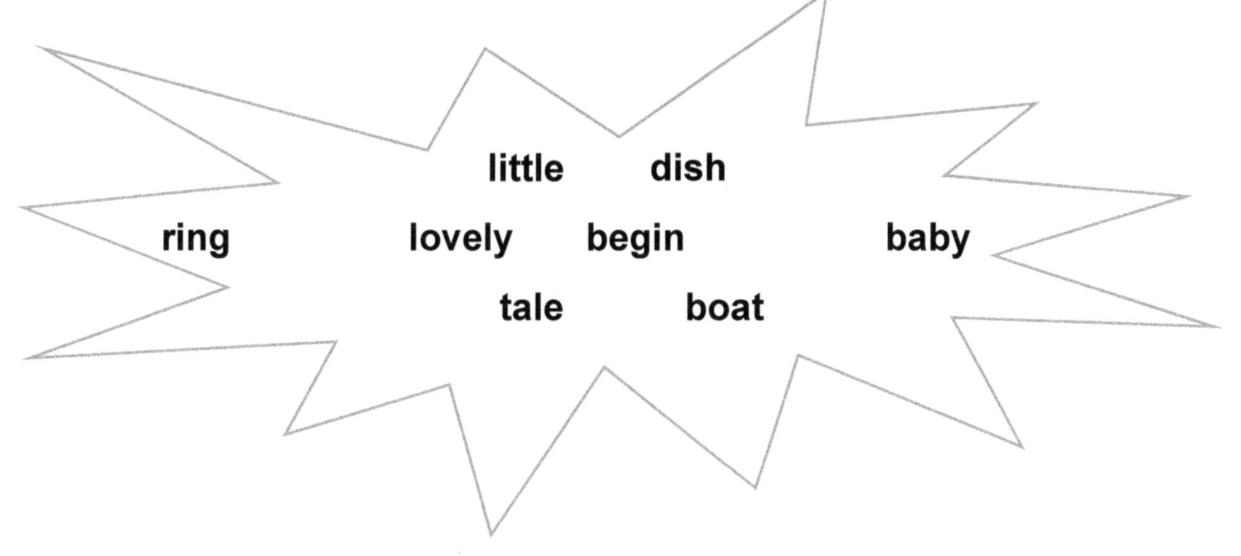

Ship - _______________

Circle - ______________

3] Bowl - ______________

4] Child - ______________

Story - ______________

Small - _______________

Pretty - _______________

Start - _______________

'a' sound

-at   -ap

__________   __________

__________   __________

__________   __________

__________   __________

__________   __________

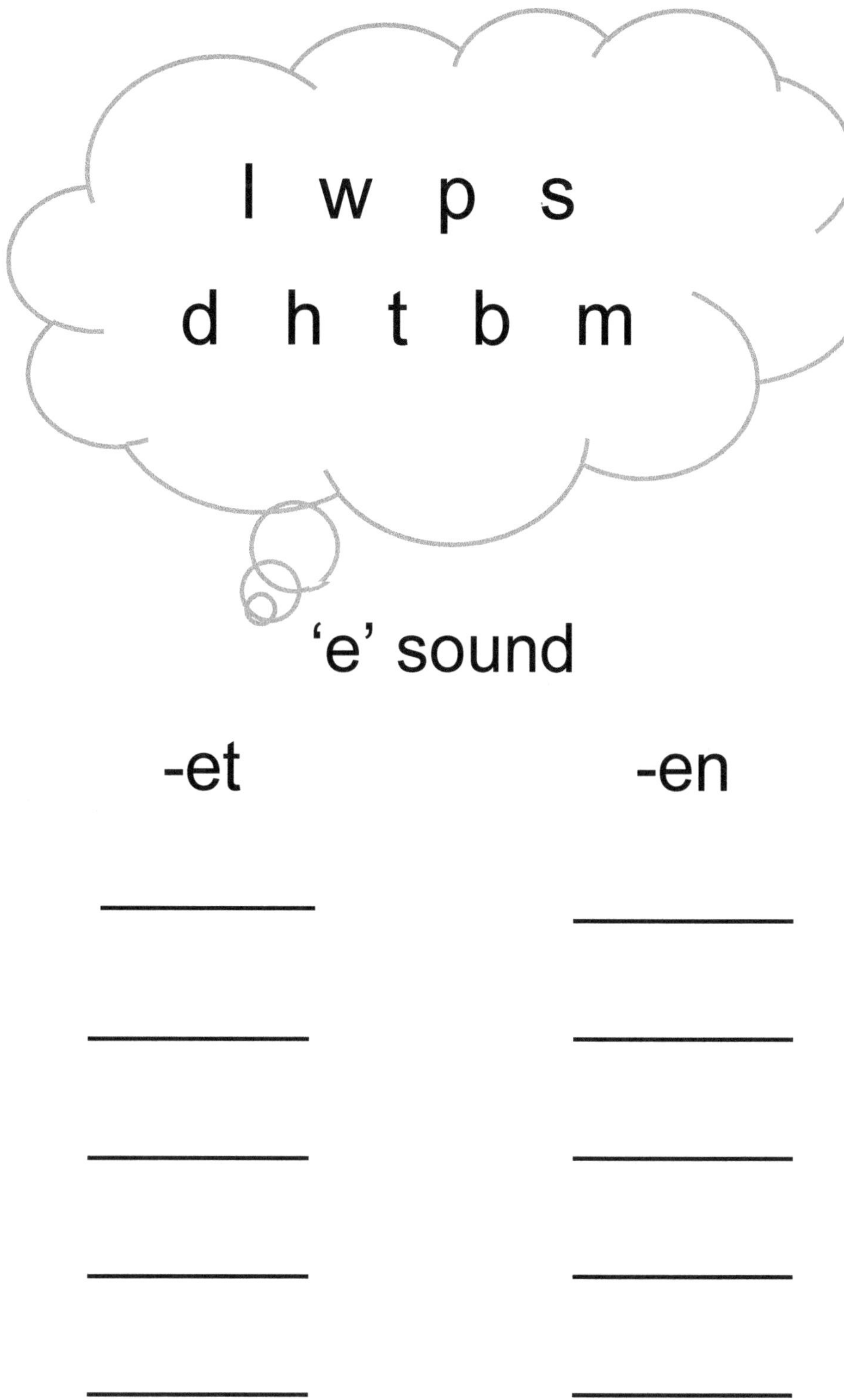

'e' sound

-et   -en

a b c d e f g h i j k
l m n o p q r s t u
v w x y z

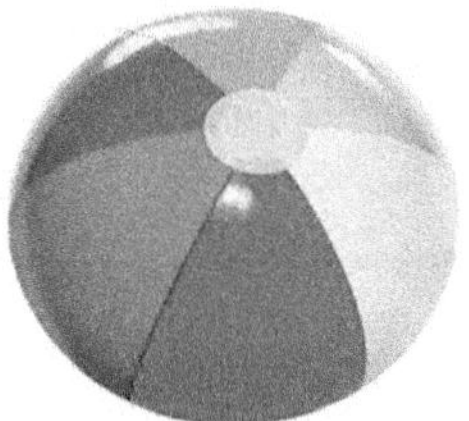

__________ is a ball.

__________ is a dog. 

________ is a bus

4.______ is a dustbin.

5. ________ is a fish.

______ is an apple.

7.______ is a mango.

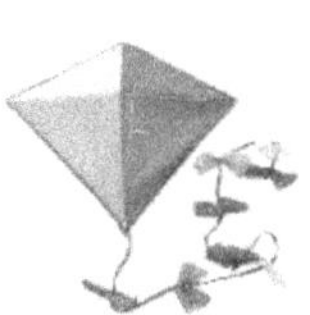

________ is a kite.

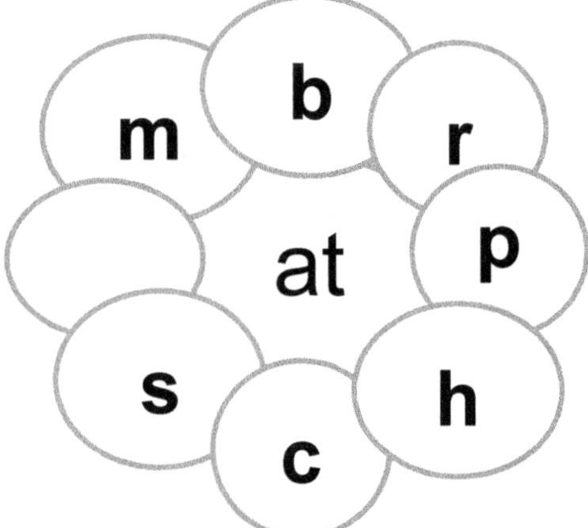

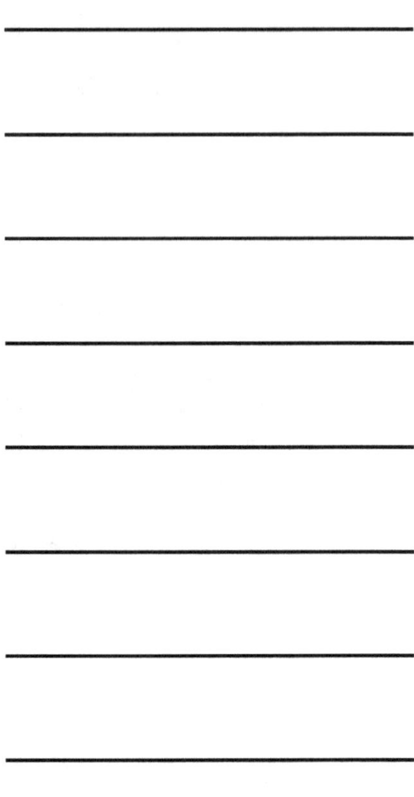

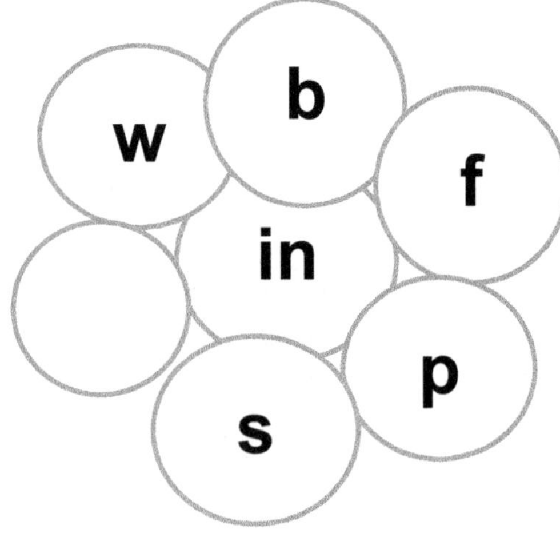

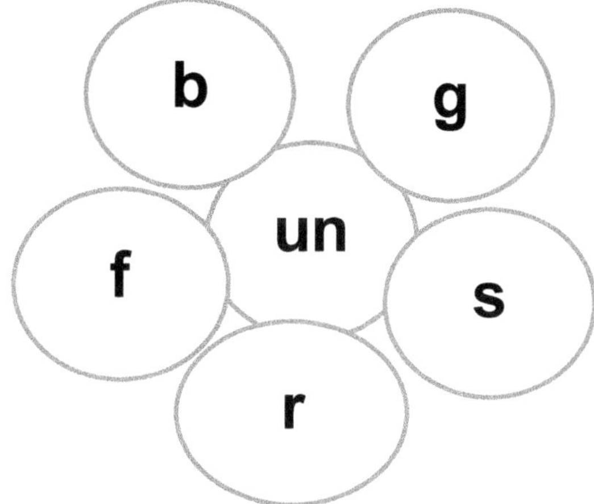

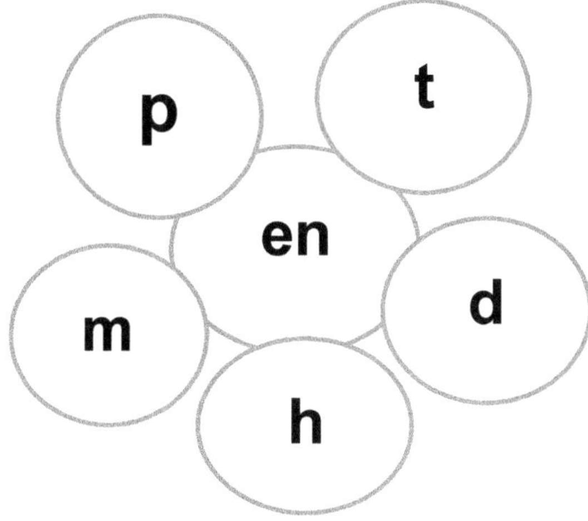

hot, down, cold]

___________ x ___________

___________ x ___________

___________ x ___________

___________ x ___________

_______ x _________

_________ x _________

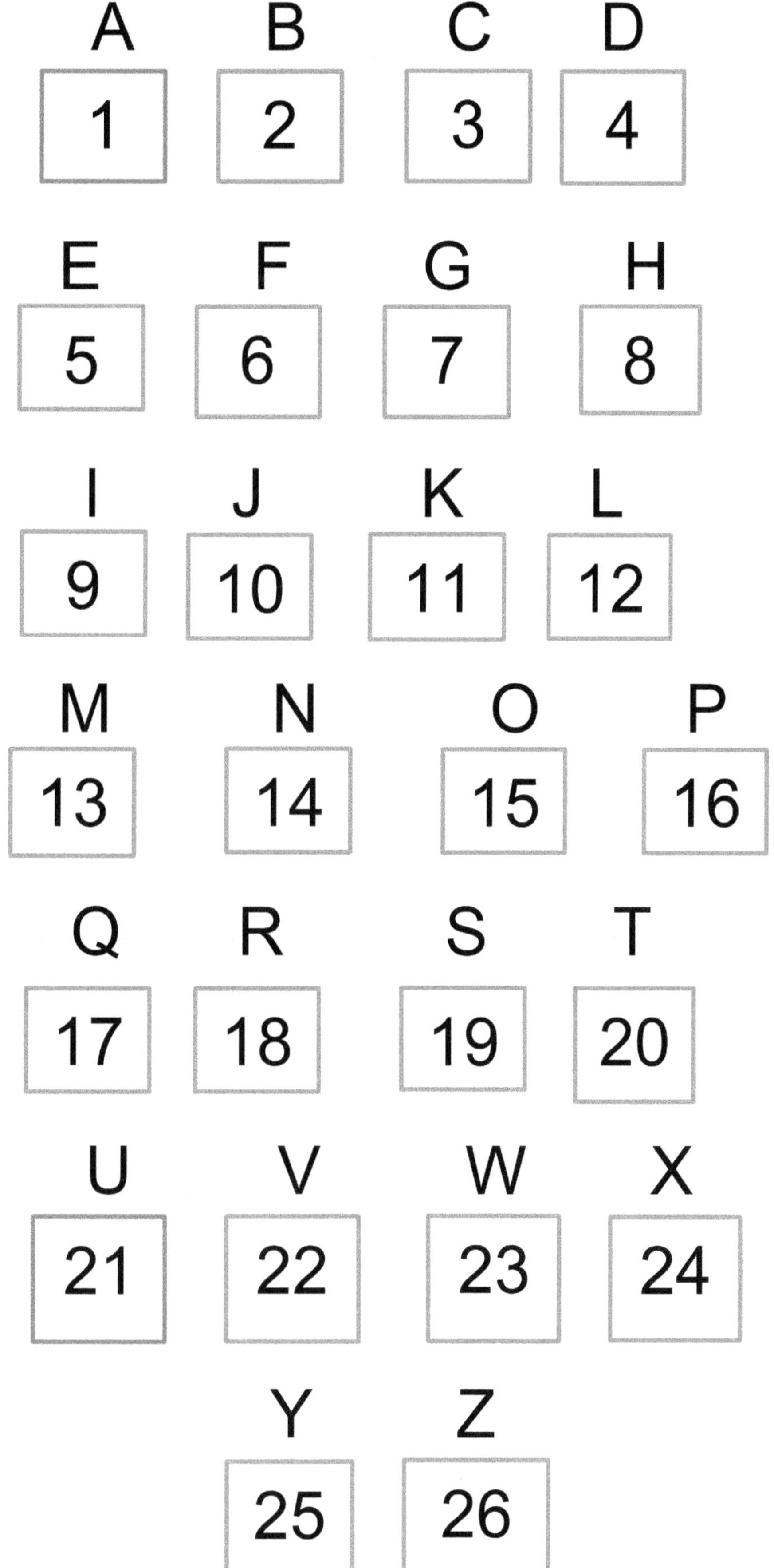

A 1
B 2
C 3
D 4
E 5
F 6
G 7
H 8
I 9
J 10
K 11
L 12
M 13
N 14
O 15
P 16
Q 17
R 18
S 19
T 20
U 21
V 22
W 23
X 24
Y 25
Z 26

For.Example: <u>B</u>   <u>A</u>   <u>B</u>   <u>A</u>   <u>N</u>
               2   1   2   1   14   1

___________   ___________   ___________   ___________   ___________
     1   16   16   12   5

___   ___   ___   ___   ___
  13   1   14   7   15

___   ___   ___   ___   ___   ___
  7   18   1   16   5   19

__   ___   ___   ___   ___   ___   ___   ___   ___
 16   9   14   5   1   16   16   12   5

___   ___   ___   ___   ___   ___
  16   1   16   1   25   1

A B C D E F G H I J K L M N O P

B , A , D ,C

Ans._______________________

F, G , E , H

Ans._______________________

M , P, N , O

Ans._______________________

J, L , K , I

Ans._______________________

box :-

{Lion, Pencil, Delhi, Elephant, Ball, Fox, Eraser, Tiger, Books, Dog, Bottle, John, School, Teacher, Mother, Park, Jungle, King, Baker, Mumbai}

Name	Place	Animal	Thing

= a   = c   = m   = b   = g

= u   = f   = o   = r   = t

+   +   = **<u>bat</u>**

+   +   =________

+   +   =________

+   +   =________

+   +   =________

+   +   =________

+   +   =________

+   +   =________

+   +   =________

CED FOUNDATION
2018

VivaVideo

acharya chanakya
शिक्षाविद सम्मान 2020
OFFICIAL ATTEMPT

www.ingramcontent.com/pod-product-compliance
Lightning Source LLC
La Vergne TN
LVHW080613200726
843509LV00007B/301